Bumpy and Boo Visit the Eye Doctor
Guess Who Needs Glasses?®

Story by Sheri Manson   Illustrations by Marcela Cabrera

To my family

For their continuous love and support in all of my endeavors.

— Sheri Manson

To my parents

For giving me the talent and the tools to be an artist. Without your love and support I wouldn't be where I am today. I love you!

— Marcela Cabrera

Merry Lane Press, a children's book publisher, educates, entertains, and expands children's understanding of the world in which they live.

Merry Lane Press also encourages our family of talented individuals to explore new horizons and embrace new ideas.

Story Copyright © 2006 Sheri Manson
Illustrations Copyright © 2006 Marcela Cabrera

Library of Congress Control Number: 2005938787

ISBN 0-9744307-3-0

Printed in China

For more information about our books, and the authors and artists who create them, e-mail us at: alan@merrylanepress.com, or visit our website: www.merrylanepress.com.

Merry Lane Press, 18 E. 16th Street, New York, NY 10003

Children are small people with big feelings and perceptions. Based on their limited experiences, however, they have fears about the unknown. How does one explain what a visit to the eye doctor entails without scaring them? In this book, Sheri Manson explains the process in a way that children can relate to, allaying their fears about glasses while addressing their concerns. The illustrations by Marcela Cabrera add fun and whimsy. Every parent should read this book to their child before they visit the eye doctor.

Norman B. Medow, M.D. F.A.C.S.
Director, Pediatric Ophthalmology & Strabismus
Manhattan Eye, Ear & Throat Hospital
New York, NY

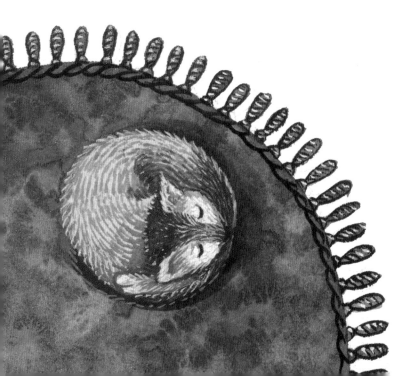

Bumpy and Boo were twins. They looked exactly alike. Even their parents got them mixed-up—especially at bath time.

Bumpy and Boo liked looking the same. They liked dressing alike when they felt like it and differently when they did not. Being an identical twin was special.

In the mornings, Boo was always the first one to wake up and put on his superhero costume. He hid next to Bumpy's bed. When Bumpy threw off his covers, Boo jumped up and yelled, "Boo!"

"AGHHH!" Bumpy screamed. "Why do you always do that to me?"

"Because you never see me," said Boo. "C'mon. Today's our class field trip to the eye doctor, and mom's coming, too."

Bumpy followed Boo. He bumped into the wall. "Ouch!" Bumpy mumbled. "Who moved the bathroom door?"

"Hey, Bump! Hey, Boo!" yelled Sarah when Bumpy and Boo arrived at school. "Race you to class!"

"On your mark, get set, go!" yelled Boo. They all ran as fast as they could. Bumpy squinted at the numbers on the classroom doors. Which one was his class?

"I win!" shouted Sarah as Bumpy crashed into his teacher, Miss Hannah.

Miss Hannah gave all the children name-tags before they boarded the school bus.

"No switching name-tags on me, Boo," Miss Hannah said to Bumpy. "You hear me?"

"Yes, Miss Hannah," said Bumpy, "but I'm not Boo," said Bumpy, as he stuck his name-tag on upside down.

"Poor Bumpy," said Sarah, turning his name-tag right side up.

"Wow! This is so cool!" Boo said, wandering around the eye doctor's office.

"Look at those little symbols on that chart," said Sarah. "I wonder what they're for?"

Bumpy squinted to see what Sarah was looking at. Was there a parrot? Or was it a dinosaur? It was blurry.

"What is the eye doctor going to do to my eyes?" whispered Bumpy. Before Boo could answer, a man said, "Hi. I'm Doctor Grant. I am an ophthalmologist. I examine your eyes to make sure you are seeing the best you can. Each of you will get a turn to use these eye paddles to cover each eye. Then we are going to put some drops into your eyes. You may feel a little sting, but they won't hurt," said Dr. Grant. "How about you first?" he said to Boo.

Boo had a huge smile on his face as he sat in the chair facing the chart.

"OK. Let's start your exam," said Dr. Grant. "Don't worry, it's fun and it won't hurt."

Dr. Grant handed Boo an eye paddle. "Put this over your left eye and tell me what you see on the top line of the chart."

"Horseback rider, butterfly, zebra, flower," said Boo.

"Now switch eyes and tell me what you see on the second line."

"Flower, zebra, horseback rider, butterfly," said Boo.

Boo felt very grown up, answering all the questions. Then Dr. Grant put drops in Boo's eyes and looked into them. Finally, Dr. Grant said to Boo, "You did it! Now wasn't that easy?"

"It sure was," said Boo. "Do I get eyeglasses now?"

"You have 20/20 vision. That means you see things very well. It also means you don't need glasses."

"Oh," said Boo, feeling a little disappointed.

Bumpy was next. Just like Boo, he put the paddle over his left eye.

Dr. Grant began asking Bumpy the same questions he had asked Boo. But this time, he said "hmmm" a lot.

"Do you squint to see things better?" Dr. Grant asked Bumpy.

Bumpy nodded.

"Do you trip a lot?"

Bumpy nodded again.

"Hmmm," answered Dr. Grant. At the end of the exam he said, "Great job. You're almost done!"

Bumpy slid off the chair. "Guess that means I have 20/20 vision, too."

"Well, not exactly," said Dr. Grant. "You actually have different vision from your brother. Looks like you need glasses."

"Eyeglasses?" said Bumpy. "But what about Boo? He has brown eyes, too. How come he doesn't need them? Does that mean we won't be identical twins anymore?"

Dr. Grant smiled and said, "Just because your eyes are the same color does not make them exactly the same. Now go with your mom and Nurse Bunny to choose some frames."

Bumpy looked at all sorts of eyeglass frames just for kids. "Those!" he said, pointing to the superhero ones just like they had at home. While Bumpy waited for his glasses he asked Nurse Bunny lots of questions.

"Can I wear my glasses swimming?"

"No, they'll probably fall off. But you can order prescription goggles for swimming."

"Can I wear my glasses to go to sleep?" asked Bumpy.

"No, you might crush them. But you can keep them right by your bed."

"Can I wear my glasses in the bath?"

"Well, they might get all fogged up."

"Hmmm," said Bumpy. "What can I wear them for?"

"You'll see," Nurse Bunny said mysteriously.

Finally, Bumpy's eyeglasses were ready. He put them on.

"There you go!" Nurse Bunny said. "These will help you see clearly. Everything you used to do before, like run and jump and play, will be more fun. Take a look."

Bumpy looked in the mirror, then at the room. He could see Sarah waving. He could see the symbols on the eye chart. And for the very first time, Bumpy saw Boo's face clearly.

Bumpy liked looking like a superhero. But he felt strange about not looking exactly like Boo anymore. Boo did not look very happy about it, either.

That night the family went out to dinner to celebrate.

Bumpy proudly read the menu aloud. He spotted the waiter all the way across the restaurant. And when he had to go to the bathroom, he didn't walk into the girl's bathroom by mistake. His parents were thrilled.

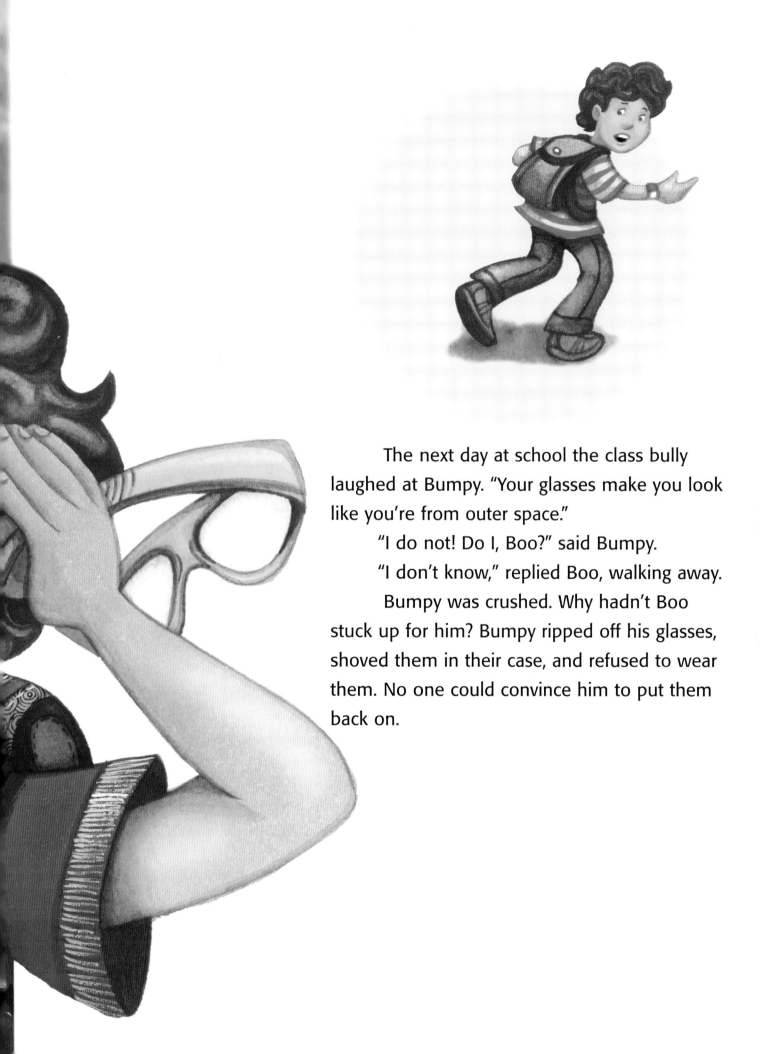

The next day at school the class bully laughed at Bumpy. "Your glasses make you look like you're from outer space."

"I do not! Do I, Boo?" said Bumpy.

"I don't know," replied Boo, walking away.

Bumpy was crushed. Why hadn't Boo stuck up for him? Bumpy ripped off his glasses, shoved them in their case, and refused to wear them. No one could convince him to put them back on.

In the playground during recess, Miss Hannah got really upset.
"Oh no! I've lost my grandmother's ring! I'll never find it in all this sand!"
The children came running and surrounded Miss Hannah.
There sure was a lot of sand.

"We'll help you!" said Sarah, wiping her glasses clean. Then she got on her knees and began sifting through the sand.

The other kids fanned out. Everyone helped—everyone except Bumpy. He could not see well without his glasses.

At the end of recess, the ring was still lost.

During lunch, Bumpy slipped his glasses back on. And he started hunting. He looked everywhere. Just when he was about to give up, he saw a sparkle inside the coat closet. There was the ring! Bumpy ran to Miss Hannah.

"Thank you, Bumpy!" she said, wiping her eyes. "This ring means so much to me!"

"It's my superhero glasses," Bumpy said shyly.

"You sure are my hero today," replied Miss Hannah.

All the children cheered. "Yay, Bumpy!"

"I wish I had glasses!" Boo said on the way home.

"Is that why you didn't stick up for me?" asked Bumpy.

Boo nodded. "I was afraid we weren't twins anymore," he said.

"We'll always be twins," said Bumpy. "And brothers, too. Even if I do have superhero glasses and you don't."

"But we won't be able to trick anyone anymore," said Boo sadly.

At bath time that night, their dad said, "It's just so great that no one will ever mix them up again!"

"Sure is," agreed their mom, scrubbing their backs.

"Wanna bet?" laughed Boo.

The twins turned to their parents. Both were wearing superhero glasses. But only one pair was real.

"Boo?" said their mom to Bumpy, then to Boo.

"Bumpy?" said their dad to Boo, then to Bumpy.

Can you tell who is who?